Plasticville

Also by David Trinidad

Pavane (1981)
Monday, Monday (1985)
Living Doll (1986)
November (1987)
Three Stories (1988)
Hand Over Heart: Poems 1981-1988 (1991)
Answer Song (1994)
Essay with Movable Parts (1998)

with Bob Flanagan
A Taste of Honey (1990)

Editor
Powerless: Selected Poems 1973-1990 by Tim Dlugos (1996)

Plasticville

poems

David Trinidad

Turtle Point Press

Library of Congress Catalog Number: 99-071392
ISBN: 1-885983-46-8

Cover and text design by Charles Rue Woods

Turtle Point Press
103 Hog Hill Road
Chappaqua, NY 10514

Printed in Canada

For Susan Wheeler

"The ultimate triumph of plastic has been the victory of package over product, of style over substance, of surface over essence."

STEPHEN FENICHELL,
Plastic: The Making of a Synthetic Century

"I want to capture the soul of plastic."

MEL ODOM

Acknowledgments

Some of these poems have previously appeared in the following publications, to whose editors grateful acknowledgment is made: *American Letters & Commentary*, *The Baffler*, *Bathos Journal*, *B City*, *Boomerang!*, *Brooklyn Review*, *Chelsea*, *Columbia Poetry Review*, *Exact Change Yearbook*, *Gargoyle*, *Gerbil*, *The Germ*, *New American Writing*, *No Roses Review*, *Pearl*, *Sonora Review*, *The Spoon River Poetry Review*, and *Urbanus*.

A slightly different version of "Clue" originally appeared in *Barney: The Modern Stone-Age Magazine* in 1981.

"Something's Got to Give" appeared in *Mondo Marilyn* (St. Martin's).

"Accessories," "Fluff," "The Game of Life," "Directions," and "Red Parade" appeared in *Plush* (Coach House Press).

"Ancient History" appeared in *American Poets Say Goodbye to the Twentieth Century* (Four Walls Eight Windows).

"Red Parade" appeared in *Queer Dog: Homo/Pup/Poetry* (Cleis Press).

"Essay with Movable Parts" was published as a chapbook by Thorngate Road in 1998.

Special thanks to the Fund for Poetry and the New York Foundation for the Arts, and to the following individuals: Dianne Conley, Lynn Crosbie, Laura Fink, Amy Gerstler, Robyn Selman, Ira Silverberg, and Susan Wheeler.

Contents

Plasticville

Something's Got to Give

A sliver of light below the locked door
alerted Mrs. Murray (the live-in
hired by Monroe's psychiatrist, Doctor
Greenson) to the grim fact that Marilyn
was still awake. It was 3 a.m. She'd
yet to shake the case of sinusitis
that had forced her—though she wished to proceed
with the film under way at Fox—to miss
a week of principal photography.
Twice she'd dragged herself to the lot, only
to faint beneath the blazing lights. Now she
lay between satin sheets—restless, lonely
and drenched with sweat. She reached for the phone. Her
insomnia was her nightly terror.

Insomnia was her nightly terror
so she gulped "bedtime cocktails": Nembutal
dissolved in champagne. Often this mixture
failed to knock her out and it would be fol-
lowed by handfuls of pills. She was always
late; sometimes she arrived on the soundstage
too puffy for close-ups. "She's drugged and dazed,"
George Cukor told the press. "It's an outrage."
The director had come to hate the star
when they made *Let's Make Love*. They had finished
only a few scenes for the new picture
and were nine days behind schedule. Against
his protests, Marilyn walked off the set
and flew to New York in a private jet.

She flew to New York in a private jet
with her soon-to-be-famous "Tinseltown
dress," which she had paid Jean Louis, her pet

1

designer, twelve grand to create. The gown
was made of "silk soufflé," the lightest and
sheerest fabric in the world, and covered
with more than six thousand shimmering hand-
sewn beads. Her scarf hid her sizzling new hair
color—a tint *Vogue* would dub "pillow slip
white." Stark naked, she'd be stitched into her
dress the following night. She'd slither up
to the microphone, squirm out of her fur
wrap, and breathlessly sing "Happy Birthday"
to her top secret lover, JFK.

Her top secret affair with JFK
ended abruptly after the gala
at Madison Square Garden. Without say-
ing why, Jack just dropped her. Monroe caught a
plane back to L.A., where she sequestered
herself in her bedroom, guzzling more bar-
biturate-spiked bubbly. She recovered
by staging a stunt that no other star
would have dared. She made sure photographers
were on hand for her sexy "skinny-dip"
sequence. As she splashed in the water, their
Nikons flashed. Then, "by accident," she slipped
off her flesh-toned mesh bikini. Bedlam
broke loose when, nude, she continued to swim.

As photos of Marilyn's "midnight swim"
bumped Liz's face off countless magazine
covers, Bobby delivered a solemn
message from "the Prez": "It's over between
us. Stop calling the White House." Then he wooed
her right into bed. Later the actress
confided to friends that both brothers screwed
like adolescents—"in and out in less
than a minute." Meanwhile, the film progressed
by fits. After a strained birthday party,

she left the set for the last time. Distressed
by what Cukor described as a "zombie-
like performance" and "deranged behavior,"
the studio decided to fire her.

When Fox officially dismissed her, her
staunch co-star stood firm: "NO MM, NO DEAN
MARTIN," read the *Herald Examiner*'s
banner headline. Drunk on wine, Monroe leaned
against the balcony of Peter and
Pat Lawford's beachfront mansion, dispirit-
edly toasting the blizzard of white sand
stirred up by Bobby's chopper. Their visit
had gone badly. Unlike Jack, he had talked
marriage; he'd lied to her, then tried to cut
her loose. As she rambled, Lawford uncorked
a fresh bottle. She'd been passed like a slut
from one to the other, so now she planned
to blow the lid off the Kennedy clan.

Alarmed, Lawford called the Kennedy clan
and warned them of Marilyn's threat. From her
bedroom window, she watched a repair van
parked on the street. Convinced the Secret Ser-
vice had bugged her line (she heard clicks every
time she talked), she'd often lug a purseful
of coins to a phone booth, her diary
(loaded with proof of her political
trysts) tucked under her arm. This document
disappeared after her alleged OD.
According to Mrs. Murray, who sent
for the ambulance, she felt uneasy
when she noticed, in the dark corridor,
a sliver of light below the locked door.

Ancient History

1949   Hedy Lamarr snips Victor Mature's hair while he sleeps, but he regains his strength in time to heave the pillars apart. George Sanders, an urbane leader of Philistines, raises his glass with rueful approval as the temple collapses about him.

1955   Condemned to wander the Mediterranean after the fall of Troy, Kirk Douglas is bewitched by Silvana Mangano, while his crew are transformed into swine.

1956   Charlton Heston turns his staff into a snake, refuses Anne Baxter's advances, frees the Jews from Pharaoh Yul Brynner, majestically leads the Exodus and parts the Red Sea, and witnesses a rather jet-propelled inscription of the Ten Commandments.

1959   Gina Lollobrigida smoulders and heaves in a series of plunging gowns, drives a chariot with abandon, dances in a curious balletic orgy, and seduces Solomon (Yul Brynner) for political purposes.

               Charlton Heston wins a chariot race and an Academy Award.

1960   Kirk Douglas excels in gladiatorial school, falls in love with Jean Simmons, and rebels after a private games staged for Roman general Laurence Olivier. Olivier makes a casual (but unmissable) come-on to slave-boy Tony Curtis.

1961   Stewart Granger rescues the Hebrews from the city of Sodom, whose depravity consists largely of dancing girls, sprawled bodies sleeping off orgies, and Stanley Baker chasing Lot's daughter (Rossana Podesta) into the tall grass. When fire and brimstone are about to descend on her palace, wicked queen Anouk Aimée is called upon to deliver the memorable line: "It's just a summer storm. Nothing to worry about." The city is then overwhelmed in splendid ruin, Granger and Co. escaping to high ground, all except Pier Angeli, who looks back and is turned into a pillar of salt.

1963   Elizabeth Taylor enters Rome enthroned on an enormous Sphinxmobile hauled by sweating musclemen. After Rex's assassination and Dick's suicide, Liz outwits Roddy McDowall by sticking her hand in a basket of figs.

1964   Christopher Plummer shows tyrannical tendencies which alarm the dead Emperor's protégé, Stephen Boyd (his hair dyed blond and marcelled), who is in love with Plummer's sister, Sophia Loren, whom Plummer marries off to Omar Sharif. Confusion ensues: the talk is endless, and there are ambushes, troop decimations, high-speed chariot crashes, and a ridiculous spear-duel between Boyd and Plummer (in the Forum, of all places), which ends with Plummer dead and Boyd nobly refusing the imperial crown. To Dimitri Tiomkin's pensive cello, Sophia prays to Vesta in a fabulous fur-trimmed cape.

1965   An all-star cast populates the Holy Land: Max von Sydow, Dorothy McGuire, Charlton Heston, David McCallum, Roddy McDowall, Sidney Poitier, Carroll Baker, Pat Boone, Telly Savalas, Angela Lansbury, Martin Landau, José Ferrer, Claude Rains, Donald Pleasance, Van Heflin, Ed Wynn. Sal Mineo is healed by Christ, as is Shelley Winters, who crieth: "I am cured! I am cured!" John Wayne, the centurion managing the Crucifixion, utters: "I believe this truly was the Son of God."

1966   Clutching his fig leaf, Michael Parks is expelled from
Paradise; Richard Harris kills his brother, Franco Nero,
in an Irish frenzy; John Huston builds a massive Ark and
potters among pairs of elephants, hippos, penguins, polar
bears, and kangaroos; Stephen Boyd (wearing heavy eye
shadow) climbs an impressive Tower of Babel and has
his language confounded; God talks to patriarch George
C. Scott.

Raquel Welch, clad in a bikini of wild-beast skins, is
carried off by a squawking pterodactyl.

Accessories

for Beauregard Houston-Montgomery

Vinyl fashion doll
comes with swimsuit, pearl earrings,
sunglasses and shoes.

*

Pastel slip, panties
and strapless bra come with comb,
brush and "real" mirror.

*

Baby dolls come with
"Dear Diary," brass alarm
clock and wax apple.

(Note: Ken's pajamas
come with same clock, glass of milk
and wax sugar bun.)

*

Sheer negligee comes
with pink pompon scuffs and stuffed
dog for Barbie's bed.

*

Robe comes with shower
cap, soap, "Hers" towel, powder
puff and box of talc.

(Note: Ken's robe comes with
white briefs, "His" towel, sponge and
electric razor.)

*

Sunback dress comes with
chef's hat, apron, four uten-
sils and potholder.

*

Blue jumper comes with
black plastic serving tray and
two soft drinks and straws.

(Note: straws are extreme-
ly difficult for Barbie
collectors to find.)

*

Turtleneck and skirt
come with scissors, needles, yarns
and "How to Knit" book.

*

Cotton dress comes with
cartwheel hat, necklace, tele-
phone and fruit-filled tote.

*

Nurse set comes with spec-
tacles, hot water bottle,
cough syrup and spoon.

(Note: "Dr. Ken" comes
with surgeon's mask, medical
bag and stethoscope.)

*

Checked shirt and jeans come
with wedgies, picnic basket,
fish and bamboo pole.

*

Brocade dress and coat
come with corduroy clutch, fur
hat, gloves and hankie.

*

Pink satin formal
comes with mink stole, pearl choker
and clear glittered pumps.

*

Leotard, tutu
and tights come with pink shoe bag
for ballet slippers.

*

Waltz-length party dress
comes with petticoat, picture
hat and sequined purse.

*

Sleek nightclub gown comes
with black gloves, bead necklace, mi-
crophone and pink scarf.

*

Wedding dress comes with
veil, graduated pearls, blue
garter and bouquet.

(Note: ring, on tiny
satin pillow, comes only
with deluxe Wedding

Party Gift Set, which
includes Barbie in "Bride's Dream,"
Ken in "Tuxedo,"

Midge in "Orange Blos-
som" and Skipper in "Flower
Girl." Mint-in-box set

is scarce and consid-
ered quite a gold mine on the
collector's market.)

Fluff

for Lynn Crosbie

O Fluff, no one knows who you are.
You were produced for one brief year
(nineteen seventy-one) after
Mattel discontinued Skooter,
Barbie's little sister Skipper's
best friend. The toy company feared
the first generation of Bar-
bie consumers, baby boomers
nearing their teens, would disappear
once puberty struck. So you were
invented, a fresh face to lure
the next wave of greedy youngsters,
pink pocketbooks full of gener-
ous allowances or hard-earned
baby-sitting money, to stores
with well-stocked doll departments, where
you were displayed, a wide-eyed, cheer-
ful, puffy-cheeked tomboy, blonde hair
in twin ponytails, wearing your
green, yellow and orange striped over-
alls. You came with a skateboard, per-
fect for cruisin' the park after
school with your pal, Growing Up Skipper.
Mattel executives were sure
that you would be a best-seller,
but your short shelf life was over
almost as soon as it had start-
ed. In essence, Fluff, you flopped. More-
over, today, when collectors
are willing to pay ten dollars
for a pair of Barbie shoes, you're
not worth a lot, even NRFB (Never
Removed From Box). I remember

you, though. As a child, I smeared your
cheeks with grease and slid you under
my girlfriend's orange plastic camper.
Barbie dolls were far too mature
for a girl like me to endure.
But not your flat-chested allure!
O tiny mechanic! The cars
I made you tune up and repair!
The engines you put together!
The windshields you washed, the batter-
ies you changed, tires you filled with air!
After work, you'd smoke a cigar-
ette, then skateboard home in the dark.
O smudged kid! O angry loner!
All my friends think that I'm bizarre
'cause Fluff, no one knows who you are.

Essay with Movable Parts

From Broadway to Hollywood, this is the fastest-selling, most whispered-about novel of the year. *And no wonder!* Jacqueline Susann's VALLEY OF THE DOLLS reveals more about the secret, drug-filled, love-starved, sex-satiated nightmare world of show business than any book ever published.

*

These tiny, whimsical characters were manufactured by Mattel from 1966-1971. Their name came from the combination of Little and Kid; thus the name Liddle Kiddles was born.

A wide variety of dolls was marketed, ranging in size from 3/4" to 4" tall. The larger of these dolls are marked at the base of their neck "© Mattel Inc." Their bodies are made of a soft vinyl material and have wires in them that enable them to bend.

Kiddles came in just about everything imaginable—jewelry, perfume bottles, lollipops, ice cream cones, soda bottles and tea cups.

*

Show business—a world where sex is a success weapon, where love is a smiling mask for hate and envy, where the past is obscured and the future is oblivion. In this sick world where

13

slipping youth and fading beauty are twin specters, the magic tickets to peace are "dolls"—the insider's word for pills—pep pills, sleeping pills, red pills, blue pills, "up" pills, "down" pills—pills to chase the truth away.

*

One of the most sought-after series by collectors are the Storybook Kiddles. These truly enchanting little dolls were created around storybook characters and nursery rhymes.

A series of seven were made: Liddle Biddle Peep, Liddle Middle Muffet, Liddle Red Riding Hiddle, Sleeping Biddle, Cinderiddle, Alice in Wonderiddle and Peter Paniddle.

*

When Pugsley abandons his pet octopus to befriend a puppy, wear a Boy Scout uniform, and play baseball, Gomez and Morticia fear their child is becoming normal.

*

The Kosmic Kiddles Series, a zany little crew of Martians, had their own spaceship to ride in and a purple plastic rock to park on. There were four Kiddles in this series: Yellow Fello, Greeny Meeny, Purple Glurple and Bluey Blooper.

*

Investigators from the MSO (Mysterious Space Objects) mistake the Addams Family for aliens while the family is enjoying a moonlight picnic and snail hunt.

*

Being an avid Kiddle collector myself, one of my fondest memories as a young girl is of my sister and me sitting on Granny's rug and zooming our Kosmic Kiddles into outer space and back to earth again. As we were tucked into our beds at night, we were reminded of the fun we'd had as our Kiddles glowed back at us in the dark.

*

Visiting dignitaries from an Iron Curtain country assume the Addamses are the typical uncultured American family. After witnessing Morticia's carnivorous plants and Uncle Fester's penchant for electricity, the officials conclude that Americans have vastly progressed in technology.

*

Player turns crank (A) which rotates gears (B) causing lever (C) to move and push stop sign against shoe (D).

*

Morticia prods the family to donate objects of art from the Addams home to a charity auction. These treasured items include Wednesday's headless Mary, Queen of Scots doll, the old flogging table, and a shrunken head. Gomez donates Pugsley's beloved wolfs'-head clock, but decides to bid at the charity auction to retrieve it. Thing's box is accidentally donated as well.

---

*

Shoe tips bucket holding metal
ball (E).

*

Meet Cathy who's lived most everywhere
From Zanzibar to Barclay Square
But Patty's only seen the sights
A girl can see from Brooklyn Heights
What a crazy pair

*

Ball rolls down rickety stairs
(F) and into rain pipe (G)
which leads it to hit helping
hand rod (H).   This causes
bowling ball (I) to fall from top
of helping hand rod through
thing-a-ma-jig (J) and bathtub
(K) to land on diving board (L).

*

But they're cousins
Identical cousins all the way
One pair of matching bookends
Different as night and day

*

Weight of bowling ball cata-
pults diver (M) through the air
and right into wash tub (N)
causing cage (O) to fall from

top of post (P) and trap unsus-
pecting mouse.

*

Where Cathy adores a minuet
The Ballet Russe and crêpe suzettes
Our Patty loves to rock 'n' roll
A hot dog makes her lose control
What a wild duet

*

She comes in a lovely dress which has a
red "velvet" top and a skirt made of
white lace over taffeta. Chatty Cathy's
pretty hair is in twin ponytails. You can
get her as a blonde, brunette, or new
auburn. There's a complete line of
Dress-Up Fashions for her, too.

*

Still they're cousins
Identical cousins and you'll find
They laugh alike they walk alike
At times they even talk alike
You can lose your mind
When cousins are two of a kind

*

One record is already in the doll, so to
make Chatty Cathy talk to you just pull
her Chatty-Ring out gently as far as it
will go (about 10 inches). When you
release the Chatty-Ring, Chatty Cathy
will talk to you!_____

*

After watching Ginger sing "I Wanna Be Loved By You" to entertain the castaways, Mary Ann, wishing she could be like Ginger Grant, falls and hits her head, causing her to believe she is Ginger. After examining Mary Ann, the Professor suggests the castaways go along with her fantasy until he can come up with a cure, advising Ginger to dress like Mary Ann.

*

When you want to turn the record over, or change the record, put Chatty Cathy on her right side. You'll see the record slot, with the lever, on her left side, like this.

Move the lever to lock position (A). Now turn Chatty Cathy over on her left side, and the record will drop out.

Put Chatty Cathy on her right side (with button still in position A). Drop the record into the slot and gently move the button back to position (B). The side of the record you want to hear should face up toward the lever.

*

Mary Ann, dressed like Ginger, asks Gilligan to practice a scene with her, kissing him passionately, while the other men dress Ginger like Mary Ann, using one of Lovey's wigs. That night Ginger serves the castaways an unappetizing dinner and later finds Mary Ann shortening all her gowns.

*

The records which come with Chatty
Cathy include:

Let's Get Acquainted (2 sides)
Let's Talk Scary
Let's Make Animal Noises
Let's Say Proverbs
Let's Make Up a Poem
    (Listen to Chatty Cathy's line—
    Then make up your own to rhyme!)
Let's Play "If I Were Mother"
Let's Be Ridiculous
Let's Be Good
Let's Pretend We're Famous

*

The next day when Mary Ann sees Ginger hanging up laundry without her wig,
she faints. Explaining that Mary Ann is experiencing traumatic shock, the
Professor decides to try hypnosis. Gilligan peeks through the window to watch
the Professor hypnotize Mary Ann, falling into a trance as the Professor tells her
she'll become Mary Ann when she hears the name Mary Ann. The Skipper pulls
Gilligan away from the window, and when the Professor wakes Mary Ann and
says her name, she remains convinced that she's Ginger.

*

Anita: I had a great collection when I was a kid. Lots
of dolls and outfits. My favorite Barbie was a redhead
with a bubble do. She had bright red lips. I loved to
dress her in her nightclub gown—it came with long
black gloves and a pink scarf. I'd stand her in front of
the microphone and she'd sing songs like Brenda Lee's
"I'm Sorry."

*

When the Skipper finds Gilligan taking a bath in his hut and mentions Mary Ann, Gilligan screams, splashes the Skipper, and chases him from the hut. Gilligan, thinking he's Mary Ann, wraps himself in a towel and runs to the girls' hut, where he finds Ginger wearing what he thinks are his clothes. After pulling Gilligan out from under Ginger's bed, the Professor hypnotizes him back to his normal self.

*

Once I got too old to play with them, I packed them away. I ironed each dress and folded them in pink tissue paper. I wrapped the dolls up, too. I put everything in shoe boxes that I taped shut and stacked in the back of the hall closet. I was saving them for when I had a daughter.

*

VALLEY OF THE DOLLS is the story of three of the most exciting women you'll ever meet; women who were too tough or too talented not to reach the top . . . and unable to enjoy it once they were there!

*

My parents divorced when I was little. I lived with my mother. As time went on, she grew really angry with my father and wouldn't let me visit him. I think she thought I saw him anyway. One day, when I came home from school, she said that she'd thrown away all my dolls. I raced outside, but the garbage men had already taken them away. All she said was: "I needed the closet space."

*

ANNE WELLES: the icy New England beauty who melted for the wrong Mr. Right . . . an Adonis famous for his infidelity.

*

Finally, I told my mother that I was seeing my father all along. That's when things *really* went downhill. On the day I turned eighteen, I came home from my after-school job and saw all my belongings on the front lawn. My clothes, my books, even my white canopy bed—right there on the front lawn! She threw me out, even changed the locks.

*

NEELY O'HARA: the lovable kid from vaudeville who became a star and a monster.

*

Rae: My parents bought me all the Kiddles I wanted. Kiddles were my life. Calamity Jiddle and her little plastic rocking horse. Soapy Skiddle and her bathtub and towel. Millie Middle with her sandbox and pail. Telly Viddle with her tiny TV set and box of Mattel pretzels. I had so many, I filled several pink Kiddles Kollector cases. I even had some in my vinyl 3-story Kiddle Klubhouse.

*

JENNIFER NORTH: the
blonde goddess who survived
every betrayal committed
against her magnificent body
except the last.

*

I have a younger cousin whose parents aren't as well-
off as mine. Growing up, she always wanted what I
had—clothes, games, books, dolls. For years she tried
to get her hands on my Kiddles. I never let her near
them. She played too rough.

*

Each of them was bred in the
Babylons of Broadway and
Hollywood.   Each of them
learned about making love,
making money, and making
believe. Each of them rode the
crest of the wave. And each of
them came finally to the Valley
of the Dolls.

*

My cousin's interest in my Kiddles seemed to grow in
proportion to my collection. The more Kiddles I got,
the more she begged to play with them every time they
visited.

*

The Brady boys are having a hard time adjusting to living with girls in their
house. The difficulties reach a boiling point when the girls want to move into the

boys' backyard clubhouse. Mike agrees that the boys should have their own space, but eventually he changes his mind, in the spirit of sharing and family unity.

*

One time my aunt and my cousin came over when I wasn't home. My mother let my cousin into my room. When I got back, I found my Kiddle collection—completely trashed! She'd cut off all their hair, written with magic markers on their little bodies, ripped off some of their heads. And she didn't get in trouble for it! "She's just expressing herself," said my aunt. "She's artistic."

Years later, she ended up marrying one of my husband's cousins. She'd met him at our wedding.

*

Someone has stolen Kitty Karry-All, Cindy's favorite doll. Cindy suspects Bobby, who had angrily told her that he hoped her doll got lost. Bobby didn't steal the doll, but he has his own problems, too: someone has stolen his kazoo. Even with that, Bobby does try to make amends by buying a new Kitty Karry-All for Cindy—but Cindy refuses to accept the present because it's not the real Kitty. Eventually, both items turn up—in Tiger's doghouse.

*

The first troll doll was carved from wood in the 1950s by a Dane named Thomas Dam, who made it as a birthday gift for his teenage daughter. It was a homely little imp with a spray of woolly white hair, a flaring nose, jug ears, big black eyes, a toothless grin, and spatulate, four-fingered hands—an effigy of the mythical Scandinavian elves visible

23

only to children and childlike grown-
ups. If one of these pixies is ever cap-
tured, he is supposed to provide his
captor with a lifetime of good fortune.

*

Marcia is devastated when she learns she has to wear braces. Even though her
family assures her she still looks pretty, she becomes even more upset when
Alan, a boy who was going to ask her to the school dance, cancels on her. She
assumes it was because of the braces. To make her feel better, Greg, Alice, and
her parents try to con three other boys into taking her to the dance. All three
show up at the Brady residence at the same time—as does Alan!

*

A Danish toy-store owner encouraged
Dam to manufacture more of them.
Known as Dammit Dolls, his comical
gnomes arrived in the U.S.A. in the
early sixties, at a time when cuteness of
all sorts was glorified—from the
Singing Nun with her lilting ballad
"Dominique" and the adorable mop-top
Beatles to 1963's number-one television
show, *The Beverly Hillbillies*. In the fall
of 1963, college coeds began adopting
troll dolls for their dorm rooms and car-
rying around miniature ones in their
purses.

*

The children have been moaning to Mike and Carol that the house is too small,
so Mike decides to sell. But then the kids realize their attachment is too strong,
and so to scare off prospective buyers and change Mike's mind, they make it
seem as if the house is haunted. When a house hunter shows up, so do two

ghosts—actually Bobby and Cindy in sheets. When Mike sees the extreme measures the kids have been taking, he realizes he can never sell.

*

Suddenly, they were a phenomenon. That same year, the belief that a troll doll provided its owner good luck was attested to by Betty Miller, the daredevil pilot who retraced Amelia Earhart's long-distance flight with only a troll doll as her copilot. Troll dolls soon became the second-biggest-selling doll of the decade, after Barbie.

*

I'm Chi-qui-ta Ba-na-na and I've come to say,
I want to be your friend to-day and ev-ry day
I come from sun-ny trop-ics where the skies are blue
I wear a happy smile just like the sun-shine too

*

Original trolls were naked, but as the fad caught on, they were sold in tunics, diapers, aprons, and sports jackets and with hair in kicky, mod colors. There were baby trolls, Grannynik and Grandpanik trolls (old ones with wrinkles), trolls on motorcycles, troll piggy banks, a complete troll wedding party in formal wear, a superhero troll in a black cape and mask, animal trolls (cows, giraffes, monkeys), and trolls to dangle from rearview mirrors in cars. At the height of the fad, a rumor spread

that if you put a troll doll in the freezer
overnight, its hair would grow.
Montgomery Ward's 1966 Christmas
mail-order catalogue offered a troll vil-
lage complete with cave, rocks, trees,
and fourteen prehistoric 1 1/4"-tall troll
villagers.

*

Golden yel-low is my col-or
My dis-po-si-tion is so sweet
Just one bite and you'll dis-cov-er
I'm a yum-my treat!

*

PARTRIDGE CARD

MOM just loves to cook for
the little Partridges.

MOVE
AHEAD 2 SPACES

*

So come dance and play and learn my song
We'll all have lots of happy fun to-ge-ther
We'll make some merry merry mu-sic
No mat-ter what the weath-er
Si-si-si-si

*

PARTRIDGE CARD

KEITH has broken a string
on his guitar.

MOVE
BACK 3 SPACES

*

Chiquita ® Banana, the winsome animated cartoon figure, was
born in 1944 and became an overnight hit as she sang her
calypso tune over the radio and in movie theatres. The song,
one of the very first singing commercials, was aired nationwide
376 times daily, making Chiquita Banana a household word
and a universal pet. She has been recreated as a doll to hold
and love. The recording is for pure musical fun.

*

PARTRIDGE CARD

TRACY is headed for the bus
on her mini bike.

MOVE
AHEAD 4 SPACES

*

When Darrin tries to surprise Samantha with an antique rocking chair, Endora—
because of a call from the antiques shop saleswoman—suspects he's fooling
around with another woman. To prove her point, Endora causes Darrin's ears to
grow each time he lies. The more he lies to keep Sam from finding out about the
rocker, the larger his ears get. Finally Sam is surprised with the chair, which

Darrin has been hiding in the Kravitzes' garage. In disgust, Endora returns Darrin's ears to normal.

*

PARTRIDGE CARD

LAURIE belongs to the
"now generation".

LOSE
1 TURN

*

While baby-sitting for Tabitha, Endora learns that she is expected at a party at the Taj Mahal. She breathes life into Tabitha's toy soldier so that it can take her place as sitter. Later, Larry believes he's missed out on a masquerade party, when Tabitha copies her grandmother's incantation and brings all her toys to life. Larry goes out for a drink with the human toy soldier, thinking it works for another agency that's trying to hire Darrin.

*

> I come from a family of pack rats and I've lived in the same house for thirty years. As my friends will attest, that's a dangerous combination. Though I got rid of many Barbie items through the years, consciously (when they were damaged) and unconsciously (when they were swallowed by the vacuum cleaner), I've also kept a variety of oddities that most women would have pitched years ago. As an adult collector, I'm thrilled. But I can't help wondering what neurotic child hung onto boxes and earrings and other minutiae some twenty years before Barbie was a hot collectible.

*

When Larry comes over to discuss ideas for a beauty account, Esmeralda accidentally conjures up Julius Caesar while making a Caesar salad, and she can't send him back. It seems that Caesar does not want to return. Sam conjures up Cleopatra to lure him back. When the client, Mrs. Charday, sees the two historic figures, she approves the ad slogan, "The Great Romances of History," for her beauty line.

*

When I packed away my Barbie in junior high school, many miscellaneous items landed in boxes destined for storage shed and basement. Who knew that those shoes, earrings, and accessories were valuable? Who knew that sixteen years later I'd be tearing my hair out looking for them!

*

Samantha and Endora take Tabitha to a live taping of the *Ho Ho the Clown* show on TV, which is sponsored by Darrin's client, the Solow Toy Company. Endora is enraged when Tabitha is excluded from the show's contest because she's related to Darrin, so she magically makes sure her granddaughter wins anyway—while on the air. Darrin then feels his career is over when Solow finds out he's Tabitha's father. Ever to the rescue, Sam conjures up a "Tabitha" doll, and claims that her daughter's TV appearance was a publicity stunt for the new toy.

*

During the last two years, I've been on a virtual treasure hunt. Combing every nook and cranny, box, case, and container I can find to see what Barbie items I might have tucked away during my hiatus from collecting. Things have turned up in the unlikeliest of places. Maybe there was some logic in putting Casey's earrings in my jewelry box. But what were a pair of silver glitter open-toe shoes doing in a 45 rpm record case with some amusement park novelties?

*

This is the doll,
JACQUELINE SUSANN,
who wrote

VALLEY
OF THE
DOLLS

which has been Number One on *The New York Times*
bestseller list for 28 consecutive
weeks—8 weeks longer than *The Group* or
Exodus—10 weeks more than *Peyton Place* or
Hawaii—15 weeks longer than *Marjorie Morningstar*!
Everything you've heard about it is true!

*

The moral of this story is don't give up the search. If your parents are still in your childhood home, comb the place. You never know what might turn up in a hard-to-vacuum corner of the carpet or that antique candy dish on the top shelf or in the dark caverns of a basement or attic. The key to success is familiarizing yourself with Barbie's accessories. Would you recognize Miss Barbie's planter without its plant? If Casey's earring lost its triangle, could you pick it out of a pin cushion? How many "Floating Gardens" bracelets have been tossed because they look like broken bits of plastic? Here's another hint. Be sure and check behind the drawers in all your cases. They're great hiding places.

*

Big, brilliant, savage, and sensational—Jacqueline Susann's
shocking, true story behind the

headlines of a glittering gener-
ation.

Jacqueline Susann's
VALLEY OF THE DOLLS

Don't miss it. And don't lend it
to a friend. You'll never get it
back.

Bits 'n Pieces

Barbie's charm bracelet
Skipper's butterfly net

(net and butterfly torn)

Skipper's ice skate
Tammy's fruit plate

(banana missing, plate cracked)

Tammy's telephone directory
Ken's car keys

(ring rusted)

Ken's camera
Barbie's umbrella

(tassel, handle missing)

Barbie's candlesticks
Skipper's cookie mix

(box crushed)

Skipper's yo-yo
Tammy's transistor radio

(antenna chewed)

Tammy's pizza
Barbie's tiara

(tip chipped)

The Game of Life

I start with $2,000 and a car.
Click, click, click . . .
spin the Wheel of Fate and

eagerly advance.
At the first fork in the road, I
decide to take

the longer way through college
with a chance
for a larger salary. *Click, click, click.*

Lawyer! (Salary $15,000)
Move ahead four spaces. PAY DAY!
On the first mountain

range, I find a uranium deposit
and collect $100,000.
At the church I stop and get

married: add
spouse, collect presents and go
on honeymoon

(five spaces). *Click, click, click.*
Many surprises
are in store for me on Life's

winding road:
win $50,000 at the race track
and triple it by

betting on the wheel; add a baby
daughter (pink peg)
then twin sons (two blue pegs);

become a sweep-
stakes winner; even take revenge
on my opponent

(sending him back ten spaces).
After I cross
the third mountain range, I

incur some
major expenses: buy a helicopter
($40,000); take

world cruise ($8,000); expand
business ($50,000);
pay $9,000 to get rid of uncle's

skunk farm.
But I keep passing PAY DAY!
and collecting

dividends on my stock. Stop
to fish on
Toll Bridge: lose turn. Cyclone

wrecks home!
(I'm insured.) Pay $5,000 for tou-
pee. The Day of

Reckoning is a breeze—no Poor
Farm for me!
I receive $20,000 for each child

and proceed.
Click, click, click. Buy phony
diamond from

best friend. Pay $10,000. This,
just one space
before Millionaire Acres!

Monster Mash

Frankenstein, Godzilla, The Blob, Phantom
of the Opera, The Wolf Man, The Hunchback
of Notre Dame, Children of the Damned, Them,
Queen of Outer Space, Creature from the Black

Lagoon, Curse of the Cat People, The Mum-
my, The Green Slime, The Brain that Wouldn't Die,
Invaders from Mars, It! The Terror from
Beyond Space, Dr. Cyclops, Freaks, The Fly,

Bride of Frankenstein, The Invisible
Man, The Mole People, Dr. Jekyll and
Mr. Hyde, Mothra, The Incredible
Shrinking Man, Dracula, The Crawling Hand,

Attack of the Fifty-Foot Woman, King
Kong, Tarantula, 13 Ghosts, The Thing.

Red Parade

Depressed because my
book wasn't nominated
for a gay award,

I lie on the couch
watching—not listening to—
the O. J. trial.

Byron, who senses
something's wrong, hides under the
bed until Ira

comes home, carrying
a bouquet of beautifully
wrapped tulips. I press

the mute button. *"This*
is your prize," he says. "Guess what
they're called." A smile in-

voluntarily
overcomes my frown. "What?" "Red
Parade." "That sounds like

the name of an old
Barbie outfit," I say. "That's
exactly what I

told the florist. And
you know what she told me?" "What?"
"When she was a girl,

she turned her Barbie
into Cleopatra: gave
her an Egyptian

haircut and painted
her nipples blue." "How cool." "Yeah,
but now she thinks that

her doll would be worth
eight hundred dollars if she
hadn't messed it up."

Once in water, the
tulips begin to unclench—
ten angry fists. Their

colors are fierce, like
Plath's "great African cat," her
"bowl of red blooms." Poor

Sylvia, who so
desperately wanted awards,
and only won them

after she was dead.
Byron jumps up, Ira sits
down and massages

my feet. "You guys." My
spirits are lifted by their
tulips, kisses, licks.

Directions

First, disconnect
smoke detectors
and dim all lights.
If desired: soft

music, incense.
Take the letters
of an ex-friend
(ten years worth) and

place them in your
kitchen sink. Douse
thoroughly with
lighter fluid

and ignite. Add
postcards, photo-
graphs, poems, notes—
any items

you might have cher-
ished as much as
you cherished said
so-called friend. Fan

the flames; let their
heat redden your
cheeks. Breathe in the
black smoke. Hold it.

Exhale. Begin
to feel unbur-

dened, free. Laugh out
loud: you've destroyed

a little piece
of that person's
voice. Scoop ashes
into plastic

trash bag. Top with
eggshells, coffee
grounds. Spit. Repeat
as needed, as

others either
betray or a-
bandon you, or
just let you down.

Plasticville

The train goes round and round
Our tiny little town

The milkman drives his truck
Up and down the block

The housewife pushes her cart
Through the supermart

The girl holds her doll
The boy catches the ball

The train goes round and round
Our quiet little town

The mailman hoists his sack
And carries it on his back

The gardener tends the lawn
Till all the weeds are gone

The mechanic works on cars
The grocer straightens jars

The train goes round and round
Our simple little town

The engineer waves hello
And lets his whistle blow

The policeman extends his arm
To protect us all from harm

41

The gentleman tips his hat
The neighbors stop to chat

The train goes round and round
Our perfect little town

The couple strolls through the park
As it begins to grow dark

The streetlights go on one by one
As the businessman hurries home

And the stores close for the day
Here in Plasticville, U.S.A.

Of Mere Plastic

for Wayne Koestenbaum

The Barbie at the end of the mind,
Beyond the last collectible, is dressed
In "Golden Glory" (1965-1966),

A gold floral lamé empire-styled
Evening dress with attached
Green chiffon scarf and

Matching coat with fur-trimmed
Neckline and sequin/bead
Detail at each side. Her accessories:

Short white gloves, clear shoes
With gold glitter, and a hard-to-find
Green silk clutch with gold filigree

Braid around the center of the bag.
It closes with a single golden button.
The boy holds her in his palm

And strokes her blonde hair.
She stares back without feeling,
Forever forbidden, an object

Of eternal mystery and insatiable
Desire. He knows then
That she is the reason

That we are happy or unhappy.
He pulls the string at the back
Of her neck; she says things like

"I have a date tonight!"
And "Let's have a fashion show
Together." Her wardrobe case

Overflows with the fanciest outfits:
"Sophisticated Lady," "Magnificence,"
    "Midnight Blue."
3 hair colors. Bendable legs too!

The doll is propelled through outer space,
A kind of miniature Barbarella.
She sports "Miss Astronaut" (1965),

A metallic silver fabric suit
(The brown plastic straps at the shoulders
And across the bodice feature

Golden buckles) and two-part
White plastic helmet. Her accessories:
Brown plastic mittens,

Zip boots, and sheer nylon
Mattel flag, which she triumphantly sticks
Into another conquered planet.

Chatty Cathy Villanelle

When you grow up, what will you do?
Please come to my tea party.
I'm Chatty Cathy. Who are you?

Let's take a trip to the zoo.
Tee-hee, tee-hee, tee-hee. You're silly!
When you grow up, what will you do?

One plus one equals two.
It's fun to learn your ABC's.
I'm Chatty Cathy. Who are you?

Please help me tie my shoe.
Can you come out and play with me?
When you grow up, what will you do?

The rooster says *cock-a-doodle-doo*.
Please read me a bedtime story.
I'm Chatty Cathy. Who are you?

Our flag is red, white and blue.
Let's makebelieve you're Mommy.
When you grow up, what will you do?
I'm Chatty Cathy. Who are you?

Clue

I was thumbing through a book from the library shelf
when Mrs. White rushed in and blurted the news
that Mr. Green had been discovered
    in the conservatory, hunched
    over the roll-top desk—
his skull smashed with something blunt
and blood trickling into a pool on the flowered carpet.
    That evening, a detective arrived from London.

He was short and portly, with a curled mustache, pince-nez
and large pipe, and he held a magnifying
glass, which expanded his face like a
    blown-up balloon. Quite a silly,
    he snooped about the hall,
joined us in the dining room,
where we were gathered around the long oak table, and then
    proceeded to question us. Miss Scarlett (cold as

a wax figure, chain-smoking): "I was napping at the
window seat in the lounge." Col. Mustard (his
monocle dropped): "Was in the billiard
    room, old bean, with Prof. Plum
    here, and scotch and cigar."
Plum (shaky): "I quite agree."
Then myself. And finally Mrs. White (a bit flustered,
    and the last one to see the victim alive): "He

ordered a tonic, sir. I was in the kitchen, sir.
Preparing the beef potpie for supper, sir."
We explained how we had only been
    asked for the weekend; nonetheless,
    he requested that we

---

remain at the mansion a
few more days. In that time, a number of grim instruments
    were considered: a butcher knife, a frayed hangman's

    rope, a small purse revolver, a rusty lead pipe, and
a heavy wrench. But all were decidedly
not the murder weapon. I spent each
    day in the study, on the plush
    sofa, observed by a
stuffed peacock as I worked on
my needlepoint. The other guests came and went, nervously
    anticipating a second death like in all

    of the pulp mysteries. Then the case very quickly
unfolded. That funny little detective
proved himself quite efficient, quite a
    scrutinizing eye: espying
    the fingerprints on the
marble mantelpiece, pulling
two long strands of bleached-blonde hair from the oval rug, coming
    across a minuscule piece of chipped nail (polished

    Camellia Pink), uncovering the secret passage
leading from the conservatory to the
lounge, where the brass candlestick (with drops
    of dried blood on its wide base) was
    concealed; then the high-heel
marks in the mud in the rose
garden; and then (the big break), hidden under the lid of
    the ballroom piano, a thick bundle of Miss

    Scarlett's gardenia-scented love letters to poor
Mr. Green! The detective surmised (at our
last meeting) that Miss Scarlett murdered
    Green in a moment of passion
    when he informed her that

47

their affair must end because
he had decided to return to his wife after a
	six-month trial separation. Just imagine!

	The wretched woman was handcuffed, scowling, and we were
given permission to leave the countryside
and return to the city. We packed
	cheerfully. Mrs. White served some
	chamomile tea on a
tray with an assortment of
delectable pastries. We all congratulated that
	wonderful detective and then chatted about

	the weather. We made plans for a future reunion
weekend. Then we were driven in a chauffeured
limousine to the train depot, where
	we departed shaking hands and
	smiling and hugging one
another like good old friends,
having removed from our faces, like stiff Halloween masks,
	and with such relief, all suspicious expressions.

Pink Poems

for Elaine Equi

1. *Emily Dickinson Pink*

Frequently the woods are pink –
Of a Despatch of Pink.
Pink – small – and punctual –
A Pink and Pulpy multitude

Is pink Eternally.
The swamps are pink with June.
Shame is the shawl of Pink
To that Pink stranger we call Dust –

2. *Anne Sexton Pink*

I wear bunny pink slippers in the hall.
Under the pink quilted covers
his face bloated and pink
with his fifth pink hand sewn onto his mouth.
Even in the pink crib
inventing curses for your sister's pink, pink ear?
The walls are permanent and pink.
The magnolias had sat once, each in a pink dress,
curling like pink tea cups
but not meaning pink, but blood and
the pink tongues and the teeth, those nails.

3. *Sylvia Plath Pink*

A workman walks by carrying a pink torso.
It is pink, with speckles.

Tomorrow the patient will have a clean, pink plastic limb.
Pink and smooth as a baby.

A funny pink world he might eat
Flickers among the flat pink roses.

The gilt and pink domes of Russia melt and float off
But he is pink and perfect.

Arabesque, Gambit, Caprice, Charade, and Mirage

Arabesque, *Gambit*, *Caprice*, *Charade*, and *Mirage*

Barbie, Ken, Midge, Allan, and Skipper

Candy Land, Chutes and Ladders, Uncle Wiggily, Game of the States, and Go to the Head of the Class

Days of Our Lives, *The Guiding Light*, *Search for Tomorrow*, *All My Children*, and *As the World Turns*

<u>Every</u> *Night, Josephine!*, *Valley of the Dolls*, *The Love Machine*, *Once Is Not Enough*, and *Dolores*

Farrah Fawcett-Majors, Kate Jackson, Jaclyn Smith, Cheryl Ladd, and Shelley Hack

Gunsmoke, *Branded*, *Bonanza*, *Rawhide*, and *Hondo*

Hedda-Get-Bedda, Betsy Wetsy, Kissy, Tipee Toes, and Teeny Tiny Tears

Inside Daisy Clover, *Splendor in the Grass*, *Love With the Proper Stranger*, *Sex and the Single Girl*, and *Bob & Carol & Ted & Alice*

Jan & Dean, Chad & Jeremy, Peter & Gordon, Simon & Garfunkel, and Sonny & Cher

Kampy Kiddle, Soapy Siddle, Telly Viddle, Slipsy Sliddle, and Trikey Triddle

Little Lotta, Little Dot, Playful Little Audrey, Baby Huey, and Richie Rich

Main Street, Adventureland, Frontierland, Fantasyland, and Tomorrowland

"Never My Love," "Along Comes Mary," "Cherish," "Windy," and "Everything That Touches You"

Old Maid, Animal Rummy, Hearts, Crazy Eights, and Snap

Planet of the Apes, *Beneath the Planet of the Apes*, *Escape from the Planet of the Apes*, *Conquest of the Planet of the Apes*, and *Battle for the Planet of the Apes*

Quickdraw McGraw, Touché Turtle, Ricochet Rabbit, Magilla Gorilla, and Huckleberry Hound

Rosemary's Baby, *The Stepford Wives*, *The Boys from Brazil*, *A Kiss Before Dying*, and *This Perfect Day*

Solo in the Spotlight, Singing in the Shower, Sweater Girl, Suburban Shopper, and Silken Flame

The Poseidon Adventure, *The Towering Inferno*, *Earthquake*, *Avalanche*, and *The Swarm*

"Up-Up And Away," "Stoned Soul Picnic," "Wedding Bell Blues," "One Less Bell To Answer," and "(Last Night) I Didn't Get To Sleep At All"

Voyage to the Bottom of the Sea, *Lost in Space*, *The Time Tunnel*, *Land of the Giants*, and *Swiss Family Robinson*

What's My Line?, *Let's Make a Deal*, *The Match Game*, *Truth or Consequences*, and *The Price Is Right*

X Y & Zee, *The V.I.P.s*, *Boom!*, *The Sandpiper*, and *Secret Ceremony*

Yahtzee, Sorry!, Perquackey, Parcheesi, and Easy Money

Zotz!, *The Tingler*, *Strait-Jacket*, *Homicidal*, and *House on Haunted Hill*

Fortunes

You are just beginning to live.
You are original and creative.

You have a yearning for perfection.
Your winsome smile will be your protection.

You are contemplative and analytical by nature.
You will take a chance in the near future.

You have an active mind and a keen imagination.
Listening is half of a conversation.

You love sports, horses and gambling but not to excess.
From now on your kindness will lead to success.

Your luck has been completely changed today.
Be direct, one can accomplish more that way.

You will get what you want through your charm and personality.
You will enjoy good health, you will be surrounded by luxury.

Someone is speaking well of you.
Now is the time to try something new.

Every Night, Byron!

Saturday

Tonight Ira went
to a dinner party
at Jenifer Berman's.
She works at *BOMB*.
I met her once: lost
it when I smelled her
cat on her clothes.
David stayed home
and watched *The
Stepford Wives* on
TV. I jumped on-
to the couch, curled
up in my favorite
throw (the fuchsia
mohair) and watched
it with him. To my
surprise, there was
a dog in the movie,
a little Jack Russell
named Fred. He
moves from New
York City (where
I live) to the small
town of Stepford
and strange things
happen. At some
point, Fred disap-
pears (actually he's
kidnapped by an
evil sheriff). This

causes his owner
Katharine Ross a
certain amount of
distress. Now, I
have to admit that
this caused *me* a
certain amount of
distress also. I stuck
it out and was re-
lieved to see Fred
alive and well at
the end of the film,
but the fact that he
just sits there and
lets Katharine Ross
get strangled by her
robot clone . . . well,
this so upset me I
jumped down and
crept under the bed
(Ira and David call
under the bed my
"den") and didn't
come out until after
midnight, when Ira
came home with
the Sunday *Times*.

Sunday

David woke up at
6 a.m. (early for him)
to go to a doll show
in New Jersey with
his friend Jeannie
Beaumont. She's

visited our apart-
ment several times.
She and David have
two things in com-
mon: they're both
poets and they both
collect old (excuse me
—"vintage") Barbie
dolls. There's a whole
wall of them in our
living room, in two
tall white IKEA cab-
inets (another poet
friend of David's,
Robyn Selman, who's
handy with tools,
helped him put them
together) with glass
doors. I sometimes
sit and stare up: the
ones with the big
bubble hairdos look
just like balls. Once
during a fight Ira
threatened to pull
off their heads and
let me chew on them,
but I knew he wasn't
serious—they cost
hundreds of dollars
and besides, David
would have been
too upset. After he
left, Ira and I slept
in till ten, then slow-
ly started our day.
My morning walk

was later than usual,
as was my breakfast
(though Ira was es-
pecially generous
with the Raisin Bran
he always sprinkles on
my dry food). Sipping
his coffee, he perused
the Business, Travel
and Real Estate sec-
tions. Then he moved
from the kitchen table
to the couch, where he
spent the afternoon
reading manuscripts.
I kept trying to get him
to throw "fluffy bone"
(my blue bone-shaped
toss 'n fetch fuzz toy
with squeaker)—to
no avail. By the time
David came home, I'd
given up and taken a
two or three hour nap.
David's packages in-
terested me at first,
until I realized they
were full of the same
old (as Ira calls it)
"Barbie crap": a shiny
black wardrobe case,
a nude red-haired doll,
and a colorful outfit
still in the cellophane.
Ira asked him how
much all of it cost.
David hemmed and

hawed: "When
words and people
fail me, I have no
choice but to take
refuge in things." Ira
didn't buy it; neither
did I. Just a high-
falutin excuse for
an expensive hobby.

Monday

I was born on De-
cember 26th (the
day after Christmas),
1991, in Glastonbury,
Connecticut (near
Hartford). I barely
remember my mother
(an extremely high-
strung show dog
named Balbrae
Katy Did) or my
many siblings. I
do remember the
day Ira and David
came. I was just
two months old—
a little ball of black
fur. The breeder
lady had already
given me a name:
Fluffy. Can you
imagine me with
such a common
moniker? When-

ever prospective
owners arrived,
she'd set us on
her cold kitchen
floor and let them
pick and choose.
Two of my brothers
had disappeared
that way, and I was
determined to be
next. So when
Ira crouched down
to get a close look,
I dashed across the
speckled pastel li-
noleum and leapt
right into his lap.
"That's the one,"
David said. "He
picked you." I
glanced up at him,
grateful for his in-
sight. And in case
there was any doubt
in Ira's mind, I
frantically started
licking his face with
my little pink tongue.

On the drive home,
I discovered they'd
chosen my name.
Byron. I later learned
it has great sentimen-
tal significance. They
had both lost close
friends (David, the

poet Rachel Sherwood;
Ira, the painter Carl
Apfelschnitt) who'd
loved the poems of
George Gordon (Lord
Byron), the famous
English Romantic.
Naturally when I
found this out I was
moved and flattered,
and made a vow
to live up to my
distinguished name.

I also learned that
I was the first pet
they, as a couple,
had ever owned.
I correctly sensed
this would give me
certain advantages.
Of course both of
them had grown up
with dogs. David
spent much of his
childhood in the
suburbs of Los An-
geles with a Samoyed
named Rashon. He
was apparently a very
sweet and sensitive
canine, and David
was devastated when
he died after suffer-
ing a heart attack
one Fourth of July.
His family then got

Skipper, a rat terrier
that turned out to
be quite a problem:
he'd bite the mail
as the postman put
it through the slot
in the front door,
leaving teeth marks
in each letter; he'd
snarl and snap at
anyone who tried
to reprimand him;
and he'd urinate
all over the house—
clearly a sign of
pent-up hostility.
But Skipper liked
David the best and
would follow him
everywhere. Ira
wasn't as lucky.
Lady, their shep-
herd mutt, didn't
care for him a bit.
It was a case of out-
right jealousy: she'd
been around for
years when Ira
came along, and
she felt the baby
stole the spot-
light from her.
Her bitterness may
have contributed to
her pitiful end: she
lost control of her
functions and ruined

the expensive wool
carpeting in their
house in the Bronx.

Tuesday

I've lived in SoHo
my whole life. It's
an O.K. neighbor-
hood, though over-
run with tourists
on weekends (this
irks Ira and David,
and more and more
I hear them complain
that it's turning in-
to one big outdoor
shopping mall). I've
always been happy
here: so many sights
and smells and sounds.
However, there is
something that hap-
pens occasionally
that really pisses
me off. But first, a
little background:

I'm a Cairn Terrier.
Over 200 years ago,
on the ancient Isle
of Skye and in the
Scottish Highlands,
my ancestors earned
their keep routing
vermin from the

rock piles (called cairns) commonly found on Scottish farmland. These early terriers were highly prized and bred for their working ability, not appearance. Such characteristics as courage, tenacity and intelligence, housed in a sturdy body clad in a weather-proof coat, armed with big teeth in strong jaws, were sought generation after generation. Today the Cairn Terrier in America is a sensible, confident little dog, independent but friendly with everyone he meets. True to our heritage, the breed still has very large teeth, large feet with thick pads and strong nails (the better to dig with!), muscular shoulders and rears, and a fearless tenacity. The immediate impression should be

that of a small, shaggy,
alert dog, head, tail
and ears up, eyes
shining with intel-
ligence, poised and
ready for anything.

Perhaps the most
famous Cairn is the
one that played Toto
in *The Wizard of Oz*.
Now, of this I am
certain: I don't look
anything like the
dog in that movie.
I'm big for my breed,
have huge ears (even
as a puppy they were
elephantine), and
since my owners
seldom send me
to the groomer, I
traipse around one
of the chicest neigh-
borhoods in Man-
hattan looking like
an unidentifiable
(albeit charming)
mess. So this is
what pisses me off.
Every now and then,
when I'm out on
a walk, people will
stop, point at me
and yell "Toto!" at
the top of their lungs.
Or they'll chant

"Follow the yel-
low brick road"
or "There's no
place like home."
Or cackle like the
Wicked Witch of
the West: "I'll get
you, and your little
dog, too!" It hap-
pened again last
Sunday afternoon.
Since West Broad-
way was mobbed
with tourists, Ira
took me over to
Thompson Street,
which was pleas-
ant to begin with.
Then, as I was
about to sniff
a promising green
garbage bag, some
queen comes run-
ning towards me
screaming "Auntie
Em! Auntie Em!"
His friends laughed.
I ignored them.

I'm reminded of
an incident that
upset David far
more than this
Toto stuff has ever
upset me. One day,
during a routine
walk around the

block, a woman
passed us and said,
"You're not going
to let him squirt on
the recyclables, are
you?" I was, at that
very moment, lift-
ing my leg on a
stack of wrapped
newspapers. David
looked at her and
said, "Mind your
own business." "It
is my business," the
woman quipped.
I won't repeat the
words they then
exchanged, but I
will tell you that
the entire affair
ended with David
and me standing
on a corner in the
middle of SoHo,
surrounded by
tourists, and him
shouting something
that only made him
look bad. I didn't
like this woman
either, but he let
her get under his
skin. Later, Ira
told him how he
would have re-
sponded to her
initial remark:

"No, I'm going
to let him squirt
on *you*." "Oh,
why couldn't I
think of a come-
back like that!"
David moaned.

Wednesday

Last night I dreamt
about Fire Island
(where I've spent
several summers):
I was running
down the beach,
on a seemingly
endless flexi-leash,
barking at smelly
horseshoe crab
shells, at sand-
pipers and gulls,
at other dogs, and
at deer nibbling
sea grass in the
dunes. I was to-
tally at one with
nature, with my
own nature, when
suddenly the sun-
ny sky turned dark
and I was a puppy
again, playfully
biting into the
cord of a floor
lamp and getting

the electrical shock
of my life. I let
out a bloodcur-
dling yelp. David
held me and cried.
I could have died!
This is my scariest
recurring night-
mare. I must have
been whimpering
in my sleep be-
cause Ira woke me,
saying "It's all
right, little guy,"
and lifted me on-
to the bed, where
I slept between
the two of them
the rest of the night.

Thursday

This morning over
three-berry muffins
from New World
Coffee, David and
Ira discussed their
upcoming vacation.
(My begging paid off:
a flurry of sweet muf-
fin crumbs in my
"Good Dog" dish!)
They're flying to
Boston for four
days, to visit Damon
Krukowski and

Naomi Yang, who
are, among other
things, terrific mu-
sicians. I've heard
their CDs—*More
Sad Hits* and *The
Wondrous World
of Damon & Na-
omi*—many times.
You'd think I'd be
disturbed by the fact
that I'm being aban-
doned for four whole
days, but I'm not.
Whenever they go
away, Ira pays Jayne
Anne Harris to take
care of me. She runs
a pet-sitting business.
I get farmed out to
her parents, Mr. and
Mrs. Harris. They
make such a won-
derful fuss over yours
truly: biscuits, baby
talk, extra-long walks
in the West Village.
There's always a
tennis ball at their
house, and some-
body—usually one
of the grandkids—
who'll throw it for
me as much as I want.
Fritz, their cat, is a
pal of mine. He's
the only feline I've

gotten to know, and
it's been a complete
pleasure. We're
basically the same:
we eat, sleep, play,
and seek affection
from humans. Mr.
Harris' hobby is
building model air-
planes. Sometimes
when he's working
on them, both Fritz
and I lie at his feet and
keep him company.

Before the Harrises,
I used to stay with
Uncle Clutch. He's
the reason David
and Ira decided to
get a Cairn. They
looked after him
for a month when
his owners, Cookie
Landau and Gerhard
Reich, went to Mex-
ico, and thought all
Cairns would be
as mild-mannered
and quiet. Boy, were
they in for a surprise!
Clutch (so christened
because he was born
in the cab of a pickup
truck; his brothers
were Axle and Diesel)
originally belonged

to Carl Apfelschnitt.
The poor pup had
some pretty tough
breaks: first, his
mother (Scruffy
Louise) dropped
dead—right in front
of him!—while chas-
ing a car (I guess her
heart just gave out);
then Carl was diag-
nosed with AIDS
and, when he became
too sick, entrusted
Clutch to Cookie.
She'd smuggle him
into the hospital
in a wicker basket
(No *Wizard of Oz*
cracks, *please*). Clutch
was orphaned twice;
perhaps that's why
he's so detached. I
have to nip, gnarl
and nudge to get him
to wrestle with me.
We used to put him
up every Christmas.
In exchange, I'd stay
at his place (outside
Philadelphia) when
David and Ira left
town. I loved romping
through the woodsy
area in their back-
yard. Unfortunately,
the last time I was there

I came home covered
with ticks. David
really hit the roof.
Shortly thereafter,
Ira found Jayne Anne.

I have, of course,
been included in
a number of David
and Ira's excursions.
Like I said yesterday,
I've spent several
glorious summers
out on Fire Island,
in the tacky but re-
laxed community
of Cherry Grove.
I've also been to
Woodstock, Great
Neck and the Bronx,
and even went on
a three-week trip
to California: San
Francisco, Nipomo
(David's family lives
there) and Los Angeles.
On airplanes,* I flew
in the cargo compart-
ment, in my claustro-
phobic pink Kennel
Cab. Luckily they
shoved little white
pills down my throat
before each flight—
I slept like a puppy.
(David should've
been drugged as

well; his worrying
drove Ira insane.)

*Other forms of
transportation I've
taken are: taxis, rental
cars, buses, ferries
(to and from Fire
Island) and trains.
Oh, and a canoe.

I've been alone here
all day and am begin-
ning to get restless.
Earlier, I took a nap
on the couch. A loud
noise woke me: I ran
to the window and
barked. Then I dozed
on the lambswool
blanket on the bed,
in a blissful sunspot,
until David's phone
rang. After the beep,
Marcie Melillo (she
sells David Barbie
dolls) left a message
saying the brunette
ponytail he wants
is available. This
should make him
happy (for a few
minutes, anyway).

I just stuck my nose
in Ira's laundry bag
(nothing new) and

checked my food
dish (still empty).
Took a sip of water.

Two tulip petals
fell on the Saarin-
en coffee table in
the living room.

Though I prefer the
companionship of
humans, I manage
to maintain a modest
social life. I've al-
ready mentioned
Uncle Clutch. In
California, I met
Gina and Max (Amy
Gerstler and Ben-
jamin Weissman's
dogs) and Rita and
Spunky (the Trin-
idad's Doberman
and Pit Bull, respec-
tively). On Fire Island
there was Cagney
(an elderly Westie),
Helga, Zooey, and
another Max. Here
in Manhattan there's
Lizzy (Robyn Selman
and Stacey D'Erasmo's
Cocker Spaniel; she
was also named after
a great poet: Elizabeth
Bishop), Macho (a
Wirehair that lives

on Wooster; he barks
at me from his third-
story window and
I, needless to say,
bark back) and Mazie
(the old Golden Re-
triever at the florist).
My other canine
acquaintances in-
clude River, Aspen,
Zephyr, Jupiter . . . .

At last! Footsteps
on the stairs! I
thought this after-
noon would never
end! I wonder which
one it is. I hope it's
Ira—he takes me
for better walks.
I'm so excited I'm
shaking myself,
shaking myself. The
key's in the lock!

Friday

Things got off to
a raucous start
today. When Ira
tried to pull me
out of my den, I
growled so fiercely
I even scared my-
self. Can't say
I didn't deserve

the smack I got.
I thought he was
going to give me
a bath, but it was
only a false alarm.
When it comes to
activities which
resemble medieval
torture, baths are
at the top of the
list. Right up there
with walks in the
pouring rain. Both
leave me wet and
shivering, not to
mention humil-
iated and dejected.
Anyway, my mood
improved when
David let me lick
his face after he
finished shaving
(I love the taste
of menthol Edge).
Then, as he was
getting dressed, he
said the magic words:
"Wanna go to the
office?" I practically
did somersaults. It's
the high point of
my week; David
goes into Ira's office
every Friday to do
the bookkeeping and
brings me with him.
A brisk five-minute

walk: down Spring
to 6th Avenue, right
to Charlton, left to
Varick, right, then
right again into the
lobby of 180, wait
for the elevator, up
ten floors, left, left,
through the door,
run to the corner
desk, and there she
is: Dianne Conley,
Ira's Marketing
Manager, one of my
favorite people in
the whole world.
I greeted her with
yips and kisses.
That's when I no-
ticed the bandage
on her hand. She
told David what
happened. Turns
out Dianne has been
feeding Jenifer Ber-
man's cat while
Jenifer is away at
a writers colony.
Well, last night
the cat went com-
pletely bonkers—
fur standing straight
up like its tail was
stuck in an electric
socket, hissing like
a little demon—and
viciously attacked

her—for no reason
at all. That darn cat!
I sensed something
was wrong with it
that time I smelled
Jenifer's jeans. Poor
Dianne ended up
in an emergency
room, had to have
a tetanus shot and
several stitches. I
felt so bad for her.
Plus she couldn't
play with me like
she usually does.
Thank God Katja
Kolinke, the sweet
intern from Ger-
many, was there. I
fished a paper cup
out of a wastebasket
and convinced her
to throw it again
and again and again.
Before I knew it, it
was time to go home.
It was already dark
outside. I proudly
led the three of us—
me, Ira and David—
one for-the-most-part-
happy little alternative
family, through the
streets of SoHo on
a Friday night. I was
still feeling pretty
frisky, but both of

them seemed tired.
They had their din-
ner delivered from
Il-Corallo (the usual:
Insalata Arcobaleno
and Pizza 4 Formaggi,
of which David fed
me a meager piece
of cheeseless crust)
and watched *The
X-Files* (too bizarre
for me) on TV. After-
wards, Ira came into
the bedroom to read.
I joined David in the
living room. He
stretched out on the
couch and watched
two episodes of *The
Mary Tyler Moore
Show* on "Nick at
Nite." Then he read
a few chapters of *The
Love Machine*. Then
wrote in his notebook
for a while. Then
turned the TV back
on and watched two
movies in a row: *Son
of Fury* (an engrossing
revenge epic from the
forties starring Tyrone
Power, Gene Tierney
and Frances Farmer)
and *The Hidden Room*
(a very effective Brit-
ish suspenser about

a possessive husband
who devises an ingen-
ious plan to kidnap
and murder his wife's
lover). In the latter, a
nimble white poodle
named Monty is also
held captive and, in the
film's thrilling climax,
single-handedly saves
the day. Satisfying to
see a dog play such an
important role. David
reached for the remote
control and clicked off
the TV. "C'mon, B.,"
he said. "Let's go to
bed." I followed him,
slid into my den, and
fell asleep thinking of
all the silly nicknames
I've had to endure: B.,
Ronie (rhymes with
"phony"), Byronie,
Ronus (rhymes with
"bonus"), Little Goober
(they got that from
David's father) and
the less formal Goob or
Goobus, Grunty Kisser
and Grunty Licker,
Squeaky Yawner, Sock
Thief, Tilty Head,
Stinky Maroo, Licky
Loo, Nipper, Nestler,
Chien Lunatique (after
one of their trips to

Paris), and (Ira at his
wittiest) Cairn Terror-
ist. But mostly they
say Byron: "We love
you—every morning
. . . *every* night, Byron!"

The Love Machine

Robin dug blondes, clean and bright, slim and hard.
"Only cows need boobs!"
But her breasts *were* sagging and her thighs were getting loose.
It was so bad it was almost high camp.
No wonder the poor bastard couldn't come.

"She's living up to her title: the Celebrity Fucker."
"Then stop shooting the breeze up my ass about sentiment."
"Oh, the title is real, but she's a broad."
"No, not even a broad—you're a rough, no-talent cunt."
"Eager to make love to you," he said.

Well, she was a good-natured nympho—and he sure as hell couldn't
    hump her more than twice a week.
"And she turns out to be the worst double-crossing cooze around."
"Sashaying off and leaving me in the crapper."

"They even hint there's something funny going on between them—
    you know: Queersville."
He had personality problems but he was not a fag!
"*Everything*, darling—orgies, and also that he's AC-DC."

"Luv, you may *just* have to have an affair with me and get me back to
    being a happy well-adjusted homosexual."
"Okay, now dive."
Valentino had outdone himself on this one: the silk blouse buttoned
    down the front, nothing had to go over the head, and she had
    those marvelous individual false eyelashes—no worry about
    the stripped ones coming off.
Everything she wore was designed for her trade.

"My real feat was learning to hold the lipstick without letting my hand shake."

A transvestite.

Chuck was a golf pro, twenty-eight, blond.

"He likes to dress like a woman and go out cruising to pick up a *guy*."

It was safer to get a hooker for sex or even jerk off.

"No tits!"

"Everyone has their own kind of loneliness," Robin said.

In My Room

I listened to "Walk Right In." I listened to
"Walk Like A Man" and "The End Of The World." I
listened to "He's So Fine" and "I Will Follow
     Him." I listened to

"Surfin' U.S.A." I listened to "It's My
Party" and "One Fine Day." I listened to "Surf
City" and "Wipe Out" and "Judy's Turn To Cry."
     I listened to "My

Boyfriend's Back." I listened to "Sally, Go 'Round
The Roses" and "Sugar Shack." I listened to
"Surfer Girl" and "Little Deuce Coupe" and "Be True
     To Your School" and "In

My Room." I listened to "You Don't Own Me." I
listened to "I Want To Hold Your Hand" and "I
Saw Her Standing There." I listened to "She Loves
     You." I listened to

"Dawn (Go Away)" and "Navy Blue." I listened
to "I Only Want To Be With You" and "Please
Please Me" and "Fun, Fun, Fun" and "Glad All Over"
     and "Can't Buy Me Love."

In my room I listened to "Do You Want To
Know A Secret." I listened to "Love Me Do"
and "P.S. I Love You." I listened to "My
     Boy Lollipop" and

"Chapel Of Love." I listened to "Don't Let The
Sun Catch You Crying." I listened to "I Get

Around" and "Don't Worry Baby." I listened
    to "Rag Doll" and "The

Little Old Lady (From Pasadena)." I
listened to "Where Did Our Love Go." I listened
to "A Hard Day's Night" and "And I Love Her." I
    listened to "The House

Of The Rising Sun" and "Oh, Pretty Woman."
I listened to "Baby Love" and "Leader Of
The Pack." I listened to "You've Lost That Lovin'
    Feelin'." I listened

to "Downtown" and "This Diamond Ring" and "King Of
The Road." I listened to "The Birds And The Bees"
and "Ferry Cross The Mersey" and "Can't You Hear
    My Heartbeat" and "Eight

Days A Week" and "Stop! In The Name Of Love." I
listened to "I'm Telling You Now" and "I Know
A Place." I listened to "Mrs. Brown You've Got
    A Lovely Daughter."

In my room I listened to "Ticket To Ride"
and "Help Me, Rhonda." I listened to "It's Not
Unusual" and "Back In My Arms Again."
    I listened to "Do

The Freddie" and "Yes, I'm Ready" and "Cara,
Mia" and "What The World Needs Now Is Love." I
listened to "Mr. Tambourine Man" and "This
    Little Bird" and "What's

New Pussycat" and "I Like It Like That" and
"I'm Henry VIII, I Am." I listened
to "Satisfaction." I listened to "Don't Just
    Stand There" and "Baby,

I'm Yours" and "Sunshine, Lollipops And Rainbows"
and "Save Your Heart For Me." I listened to "Hold
Me, Thrill Me, Kiss Me" and "Unchained Melody."
    I listened to "I

Got You Babe" and "Down In The Boondocks" and "You
Were On My Mind" and "It's The Same Old Song." I
listened to "California Girls" and "Help!" and
    "Nothing But Heartaches."

In my room I listened to "All I Really
Want To Do" and "It Ain't Me Babe" and "Eve Of
Destruction." I listened to "Catch Us If You
    Can" and "Summer Nights."

In my room I listened to "Hang On Sloopy."
I listened to "You've Got Your Troubles" and "Do
You Believe In Magic" and "Home Of The Brave"
    and "Baby Don't Go."

In my room I listened to "Yesterday." I
listened to "A Lover's Concerto" and "Make
Me Your Baby" and "You're The One" and "Every-
    body Loves A Clown."

In my room I listened to "Get Off Of My
Cloud." I listened to "Roses And Rainbows" and
"1-2-3" and "Let's Hang On!" and "Rescue Me."
    I listened to "I

Hear A Symphony." I listened to "Turn! Turn!
Turn!" and "I Can Never Go Home Anymore"
and "Over And Over." I listened to "The
    Sounds Of Silence" and

"You Didn't Have To Be So Nice." I listened
to "We Can Work It Out" and "Day Tripper" and

"As Tears Go By" and "Lies." I listened to "My
    Love" and "Lightnin' Strikes."

In my room I listened to "California
Dreamin'" and "These Boots Are Made For Walkin'" and
"Elusive Butterfly" and "Working My Way
    Back To You" and "You

Baby" and "Kicks" and "Shake Me, Wake Me (When It's
Over)." I listened to "Time Won't Let Me" in
my room. I listened to "Monday, Monday" in
    my room, in my room.

Fat Liz / Bad Anne

for Jeffery Conway

"167 Pounds! That's a lotta Liz."
  —*National Enquirer*

". . . ultimately she did not find time enough
for that final perfection."
            —Linda Gray Sexton

. . . food, at least, seemed an innocent indulgence, and in the early
months of 1956, she ate with alarming abandon: she had already
gained weight during her second pregnancy, and now the pounds
quickly accumulated. "My taste buds get in an uproar," she said, "and
I get a lusty, sensual thing out of eating." Montgomery Clift was con-
cerned about the effect on her health: "She really became terribly
overweight," he said, "and when she came out in an evening dress, I
said, 'Honey, you're the broadest broad I ever saw!'" Her reaction was
wild laughter.

> *I want mother's milk,*
> *that good sour soup.*
> *I want breasts singing like eggplants,*
> *and a mouth above making kisses.*

She ordered chili flown over from Chasen's in Los Angeles, stone
crabs from the coast of Florida, smoked salmon from Barney
Greengrass in New York, sirloin steaks from Chicago, shrimp creole
from New Orleans, spare ribs from St. Louis, white asparagus from the
French countryside, fresh linguini from Genoa.

> *I want nipples like shy strawberries*
> *for I need to suck the sky.*

Installed in her fourteen-room "home away from home," Taylor behaved in the grandest of manners. Small trucks from Rome's gourmet grocery stores zipped in and out of the gates, bearing delicacies that cost at least $150 per day. The liquor bill alone ran over $500 per week.

The two Italian butlers, veterans in service to princes and dukes, were often frazzled by the star's imperious ways. She insisted that everything at dinner be color-coordinated—flowers, napkins, candles and tablecloths—all to match whatever gown she might choose for dinner.

> *I need to bite also*
> *as in a carrot stick.*
> *I need arms that rock,*
> *two clean clam shells singing ocean.*

Elizabeth, never out of sight, turned up at the shooting location each day at noontime with a picnic hamper and bottles of wine. Her bikinis were vivid, and she kidded herself as a love goddess. Well might she have such a sense of humor about herself that season, for—idle and inclined to eat and drink too much—she was swiftly gaining weight: the bikinis looked tinier and more tragicomical by the day. "Look at her," said Richard acidly more than once. "She walks and looks just like a French tart."

> *Further I need weeds to eat*
> *for they are the spinach of the soul.*

Elizabeth was outfitted mostly in caftans, and when she was not, a change in her appearance was at once evident: whereas before there was an occasional slight dumpiness to her young figure, she was now downright overweight, and long hair, careful lighting and flowing gowns could not conceal the fact.

I am hungry and you give me
a dictionary to decipher.
I am a baby all wrapped up in its red howl
and you pour salt into my mouth.

. . . at La Strega, a popular restaurant in the village of Practica de Mare . . . she held forth on whatever struck her fancy, and she ordered for herself and everyone at her table enormous portions of spaghetti with whiskey sauce, potatoes with coddled eggs and crepes with lemon cream . . . . Visiting reporters had the impression that Elizabeth was dedicated to self-indulgence: pounds of caviar and cases of champagne arrived at her villa in vulgar profusion and were quickly consumed.

Your nipples are stitched up like sutures
and although I suck
I suck air
and even the big fat sugar moves away.

By midsummer, some reporters observed that despite Elizabeth's strenuous socializing and late-night dancing, she seemed heavier than ever. The truth was, as she later admitted, that in private she had turned to food and drink for comfort. And if late-night snacking and tippling did not induce sleep, it was easy to find doctors to prescribe sedatives and hypnotics. What physician, anywhere, would refuse to make Elizabeth Taylor happy?

Tell me! Tell me! Why is it?
I need food
and you walk away reading the paper.

"I enjoy eating and I love to cook," she said defensively. "Eating is one of the great pleasures of life—but I can hardly get into my clothes."

Evening Twilight

Of sea and wind, and through the deepening gloom
These days are short, brittle; there is only one night.
Waxing and waning in the fog of the room,
You look like a lovely ship taking to flight

O'er the land. He considered his honeydew
As softly as falling-stars come to their ends
Against the church walls across the street. Two
Goes out drinking with four male college friends.

I remember "Howdy Doody" and "Queen for a Day."
Because it just happened a few minutes ago.
What I wanted to do was to find a way
Along the same lines as before. Old ice, new snow.

A handsome young man, dressed all in white, carries
Future findings, silver, in the cranial cockpit,
Screens blank as postcards from cemeteries,
In a language troublesome and private.

Driving home in my blue Mustang, I threw up
On less crudely painted pictures of familiar
Things we think of will be there. He, says, *sand*, she,
  a large cup
To razor-cross the cobra's kiss, to drink its venom.
  Her slender

Avocados, plums, the more delicate grapefruit.
One is the song which fiends and angels sing:
"Keep it up," he joked, "I'll ditch you for the cute
Pink flowers borne on the naked twigs in early spring,

And the sticky sweetness of provincial tears
Like untrained torch singers under a temporary moon."
The grave and that eternity to which the grave adheres—
Hands in your pockets, whistling the same old tune?

This poem is for Robert, remember Bob? He told me my
    lover's name
And he does not forget. Danny's voice on
The stitching-frame, weaving his fire and fame,
So when you wake up and find everything gone,

I'll have to wear dark glasses and carry the cane.
The skill comes in knowing when to close your eyes.
Heard far away in the distance: "Looks like rain."
He shudders his coat as if to throw off flies.

Inside, the rare bone of my hand and that harp
From some recess in the depths of my soul.
Waving a cup of grape, smart kid, his nose is sharp,
The objects of its scrutiny: trees, blue plums in a bowl,

Lincoln Continental, ocean waves, lunar eclipse
(Which caused disorder). Something on a pedestal
In the water of each other's mouths. Lips, those lips
Shake when a shovel strikes an amber bottle

At the sound of a man's command. These macho boys
On their bicycles, in the woods, are set upon by fur
Into such a sudden zest of summertime joys
I went back in the alley and I opened up my door. All her

Hushed oars dipping and squeaking. And the five sat
    all the time
So nicely, the cane too, on the red marble. No
I never smiled much here. Farewell, colleagues of the
    sublime!
Timmy's coming back to you from Orlando—

Florida, Vermont, Alabama, Mississippi! I guess
It is all my Midwestern parents talk about any more
In this sodden world. Nobody understood my distress:
I now commenced my search in earnest, but still, as before,

I would say the writing of poems is like dancing on ice
In the crisp dark night that has no stars. And
Women's voices, hurt, weeping. Intrusive electronic
    noises. Mice
Polish over old boards where he and she stand

During the commercials and plan their future—
Fearful and corpse-like fishes hooked and being played
To "Parables from Nature," 1894—a picture
Like your mind! I love you faded, old, exiled and afraid

Of my origin. I seemed to be reaching the heights of art
Whereof Life held content the useless key;
No one may see this put-away museum-piece, this
    country cart
Going "bye-bye" for a while. My friend and companion
    informs me

There's a moth flying in circles about an inch above
All that oriental splendor of bamboo and hotel palms
    and stale
Talk of a wife. Now that I know about the fear of love
You who live cannot know what else the seeds must be.
    Hail

Poets who mistake that gesture for a style.
Stay awake, keep the film going, ignore the body count,
    it's just
Family photographs, and this is a man, look at his smile,
A movement there! As if the towers had thrust

Through the window beams from a wandering car
And he grinds his teeth gently because the world pays for
A flag discolored by the rains. In my head drums are
Surface things. Intentions matter not at all. God does
    not read your

Penny horoscope, letters never mailed. The door may
Melt where the guideless cloud melts—Oh! favored by
Bodies shining in their feathers. A half moon at midday,
I have seen it come these eight years, and these ten years,
    and I

Grow indifferent to dog howls, to the nestling's last peep;
What would I give for words, if only words would
Emerge; but you sleep somewhere, who in my waking
    never sleep.
You like a golden laugh. Idol of tacky teenage-hood,

I tell you the past is a bucket of ashes, I tell you
We put the urn aboard ship with this inscription: This
Transparent body casting long dark shadows through
The sky, in blue for elms, planted its lightest kiss

In the middle of Florence. Florence in flames. Like
The hour glass marking the passing of more wasted
    time.
I knew: the last of the coke, the dope, me and Mike
On the land spit. The sea wears a bell in its navel.
    And I'm

Anxious, exhausted, holding a luger. Grey as
A rosary of rock crystal. Wisteria blossoms. Plum
Clouds float and sheep graze. A lot of dust has
A crack at love in the warm months to come.

The quick red fox jumped over the lazy brown dog.
But note this moon. Recall how the night nurse

94

Can sometimes see it still in the shimmering smog
Of knowing?—I stand and hold up this universe

In the hush of space, in rooms of leaves. A high
      round
Snowman holding up the North Pole. Incredible!
      we'd say
Conversations. In the morning, I hear the sound
In the warm wind, delta reeds vibrating, a-sway,

The last flick of the wolf's tail as it disappears in
Something you smoke, or a telephone number. Late:
29 minutes past 3 a.m. Without flipping into a spin,
Candles on the lawn go out. You make a path across
      the slate

To escape utterly from others' anchors and holds!
The gifts do not desert us, fountains do not dry
Before the spectacle of our lives with joined hands.
      The storm unfolds
Instead of eyes. A slow gray feather floated down
      the sky.

Garbo's Trolls

Often, the reclusive
actress, then in her late
sixties, fought intrusive

sleep-robbing thoughts (her great
silent romance with John
Gilbert, for instance—fate

played a dirty trick on
him during the furor
about sound: couldn't con

"customers," her word for
fans, with a voice that high,
Adonis or not; or

her unlikely start, shy
and overweight, her rise
to fame, her quest for pri-

vacy; or her disguise—
dark glasses and scarf—and
how she'd come to despise

the press, her upraised hand,
spotted with age, blocking
her face in the newsstand

photos she passed walking
aimlessly around mid-
town Manhattan, shocking

even the most jaded
celebrity spotters)
and fought all her wretched

3 a.m. pains (doctors
were out: she was afraid
of air conditioners

so she stubbornly stayed
home and suffered) by crouch-
ing before the brocade

Louis XV couch
in her living room. "Damn
sandman," she'd mutter, grouch-

y from lack of sleep. Sam
Green sat rapt on his end:
"She'd say 'Let's go' and slam

down the phone. She could send
for me any time." Green,
an art dealer, befriend-

ed the eccentric screen
legend in seventy-
one; they were often seen

wandering the city
together. The invite
came years later. "Thirsty,

Mr. Green?" she asked right
after a brisk walk. Few
had been inside. Delight-

ed, Green followed her to
the elevator. He
took in the fifth-floor view

of the river while she
mixed drinks in another
room. Munching cocktail pea-

nuts, one fell, rolled under
the couch. He knelt to pick
it up and discovered

something odd: "A Nordic
creature . . . you know, a troll,
a plastic gnome with thick

orange Dynel hair and coal-
black eyes, peeking out at
me." Behind it: a whole

row of trolls. Stunned, Green sat
on the floor. His next vis-
it, he ascertained that

they'd been rearranged; his
theory is that "Miss G."
was on some nights so mis-

erably sleepless she
would act out little fan-
tasies with trolls. "Maybe,

when her precious sandman
refused to show, she'd stage
famous folk tales from Scan-

dinavia or age-
less scenes from her films: Queen
Christina with her page-

boy and butch velveteen
attire; pale Camille swoon-
ing in tulle; or the lean

Anna K., misfortune
prodding her off the train
platform. Maybe, by moon-

light, she would entertain
herself this way." Green could-
n't ask her to explain

her trolls, of course, but would
look underneath the so-
fa whenever he could.

He'd wait till her death, though
she dropped him, to betray
the troll secret. Garbo

walked alone, and would stay
sphinx-like and elusive
until her final day.

Notes

Plasticville is the name of a model train village manufactured in the '50s and '60s by Bachmann Brothers, Inc. Such miniature structures as gas stations, cathedrals, schoolhouses, supermarkets, and barns enhanced the realism of electric toy-train layouts. Tiny plastic people, animals, picket fences, street lamps, trees, and other accessories were also available.

"The Love Machine" is composed of sentences from Jacqueline Susann's novel of the same title.

"Fat Liz / Bad Anne" is comprised of Anne Sexton's posthumously published poem "Food" (from *45 Mercy Street*) and excerpts from Donald Spoto's *A Passion for Life: The Biography of Elizabeth Taylor* and Peter Harry Brown and Patte B. Barham's *Marilyn: The Last Take*.

"Evening Twilight" is a cento made up of lines from 116 different poems. The order is alphabetical by poet; thus the poem begins with Matthew Arnold and ends with James Wright. "Evening Twilight" is the title of a poem by Baudelaire.